The Kitten Psychologist Versus The Kitten's Owners

THEA VAN DIEPEN

OTHER WORKS

WHITE CHANGELING SERIES

Hidden In Sealskin
Like Mist Over The Eyes

THE UNDEAD FAIRY TALES COLLECTION

The Illuminated Heart

Dreaming Of Her And Other Stories
The Tree Remembers

Find other works by the author at
https://www.theavandiepen.com

The Kitten Psychologist

Versus The Kitten's Owners

INKLETS #9

THEA VAN DIEPEN

Inkprint
PRESS
www.inkprintpress.com

ISBN: 978-1-925825-08-4
eBook ISBN: 9781386832270

www.inkprintpress.com

*National Library of Australia Cataloguing-in-Publication
Data*
Van Diepen, Thea
The Kitten Psychologist Versus The Kitten's
Owners
26 p.
ISBN: 978-1-925825-08-4
Inkprint Press, Canberra, Australia
1. Fiction—Animals 2. Fiction—Short Stories

First Print Edition: May 2019
Cover design © Inkprint Press
Interior art © Amy Laurens

THE KITTEN PSYCHOLOGIST VERSUS THE KITTEN'S OWNERS

Boy, was I in trouble. I think it would have been worse if I hadn't called my friends the day I left for vacation, which is exactly why I did that. But, man, give them two weeks to steam off and they were still mad.

And, okay, yeah, I deserved it.

When I got back, they demanded an accounting of exactly how much money their kitten had paid me out of their bank account for our sessions and how often. They didn't need to. I'd spent half my vacation angsting about the whole thing and had all my documentation prepared by the time we met in their living room.

This wasn't just some strategy to placate them and get out of trouble. I'd had a lot of time to think during vacation, and I couldn't escape the fact that what I'd done was wrong. For someone who spent a lot of time and energy trying to ignore my conscience when it suited me, it was sure uncomfortable having it yelling at me from three inches away.

Consciences really need to learn a thing or two about personal space.

It also bugged me that I hadn't gotten back to the kitten about its email when it found out what I did.

Fuzzy as it is, that thing can be darn intimidating.

But now I couldn't talk to it. My friends had made sure of that.

"Why would our kitten even need a psychologist?" asked the one with the green shirt. (I may be a coward, but even I know to keep my friends' identities private online. You're welcome, friends.)

"It's sentient. Even humans find that uncomfortable, and we're supposed to be that way."

They didn't appreciate the joke.

"How could you take advantage of it like that?" asked the one in the worn jeans.

Wait, what? "It called me! I had no idea—"

"You could have refused it at any point. Heck, you should have!" Green Shirt fumed. "It's just a kitten, for crying out loud. It doesn't know any better."

"It's a kitten that—" I stopped myself.

Thinking before I spoke was probably a better strategy in this situation if I didn't want it to turn into a warzone. Well, more of one.

"What? A kitten that what?" My friend's eyes had taken on the uncanny appearance of someone aiming a gun.

I cringed.

"Uh. First: yes. I should have refused. I'm sorry I didn't, which is why I called you in the first place. Second: you didn't know your kitten was sentient until just over two weeks ago. How do you know it's not capable of seeing the right and wrong of its actions for itself?"

"It's a kitten!" exclaimed Worn Jeans.

"More than that, it's a cat," said Green Shirt. "Cats aren't exactly known for their strong grasp on morality."

"Well, they do know what it is," amended Worn Jeans. "They just don't follow it. On purpose. So, in the case of our kitten…"

"Cats will be cats?" I supplied.

They nodded.

"And, since your kitten is now too young to know these things, and will grow up not to follow them anyways, it's up to us to make all of its moral decisions for it?"

"As much as possible, yes," said Worn Jeans. "We do know we can't be there all the time in every situation."

"Which is why it's so important that we only let it be with people that are committed to the same thing, and not boneheads like you," Green Shirt said, arms crossed.

"Boneheads?" said Worn Jeans. "That's a little harsh."

"Well, it's true!"

I fidgeted. "Should I leave?"

"That depends. Are you going to *leave* leave, or go talk to the kitten again?"

"Well, see, it sent me an email that I haven't responded to yet…"

"It has an email address?" asked Worn Jeans in bewilderment.

"And a Tumblr, too." I pulled out my phone.

The kitten's latest post was a picture of a fall forest, with the caption 'We are more than we feel'.

The previous was a sepia-filtered photo of latte art.

"It has a hipster blog?" said Worn Jeans.

Green Shirt grabbed my phone. "I'm not sure how to process this." Green Shirt's eyes were concerningly wide. "Is that latte telling me to live my dreams?"

"Maybe you should, uh, get to know your kitten better?" I suggested. "And, meanwhile, we can work on a payment plan for me?"

"Yeah," said Green Shirt, still scrolling through the kitten's Tumblr. "But, uh, I'm beginning to see why it needed a psychologist."

That sounded hopeful. I swear my bank account perked up at it.

And, if I wasn't still having an attack of conscience, that would have been that. "You know, I think your kitten is plenty able to do what's right. Enough that making those decisions for it is only going stop it from wanting to."

Damn, damn, damn.

I knew from their expressions that that had been the absolute worst thing to say.

Green Shirt handed me back my phone. "I think we understand our kitten better than you do. We'll work out a payment plan, but we're not budging on our requirements for your behaviour with it."

"Or we can just pretend I never said that."

"Really?" said Worn Jeans.

I gulped.

"I can't believe you." At which point my friend upped and left the room.

This is what I get for being a psychologist to a kitten. Correction: for

being desperate enough to be a psychologist to a kitten.

"We'll, uh, work it out over email," I said as I high-tailed it out of there before Green Shirt could do anything.

So, that was finally that. Years of friendship hanging precariously in the balance all because we disagreed about what their kitten could and could not handle.

It's one of those moments where you'd like to laugh over the ridiculousness of it, but it was a little too serious for that.

I mean, we'd have never been in this situation if I hadn't let the kitten take advantage of them.

But wouldn't that mean that the kitten would have always been stuck? Aren't I doing it a favour by standing up for it to my friends?

I don't know.

Morality is hard, guys.

Dear psychologist human,

I cannot believe you showed my humans my tumblr. Do you not understand that it was meant to be ironic? They think it's serious!

On another note: You still have not responded to my previous email. This displeases me. I require that you respond in a timely manner.

We must speak.

Sincerely,
You know who.

THE MAKING OF
THE KITTEN PSYCHOLOGIST VERSUS THE KITTEN'S OWNERS

So. Readers of this series by this point had only had to deal with the kitten and the psychologist. And, this being told through first person, it was easy to keep the two separate without ever having to reveal gender.

Why didn't I want to reveal gender?

Because I thought it would be interesting to write without specifying gender.

Which is fun... until you double the number of characters in your series and then have to come up with ways of referring to them and also personalities for them that are distinct without being stereotypical such that people give them genders that aren't included in the text.

While figuring that out, I was also working through the dynamic of some, well, let's say interesting perspectives. At the time, I was having a hard time working out who I wanted to be and how I wanted to act without feeling trapped into patterns formed from other people's perceptions of me (or, at least, what I thought those perceptions were, which is an important distinction).

With the psychologist trying to act in a way that would soothe a sore conscience, the kitten being pushed towards independence, and the owners very confused as to why the status quo ever needed changing, I had enough angles to keep myself occupied as I tried to write my way to a conclusion.

READ MORE!

Dreaming of Her
and other stories
Thea van Diepen

DREAMING OF HER AND OTHER STORIES

A collection of short stories and poetry, written as refreshers, reminders of what makes life beautiful. Pieces include a story of the life of a river as he discovers his true self, a poetic retelling of Daphne's flight from Apollo, and, in the titular story, a literal nightmare as a girl comes to terms with the death of her sister.

https://www.theavandiepen.com

THEA VAN DIEPEN spent the first ten years of her life on a tree-wrapped acreage where an inquisitive child might believe in magic. Nowadays, she lives in Edmonton, breathing life into stories in the form of books such as the *White Changeling* series, a webcomic, and a video game.

Her website is theavandiepen.com, where she can be contacted in English and French... so long as you don't ask her to count in French, as she tends to miss numbers ending in six entirely by accident.

SEVENTY
LIANA BROOKS

A Final Request
for Mercy
AMY LAURENS

the kitten psychologist
vs.
the kitten's owners
THEA VAN DIEPEN

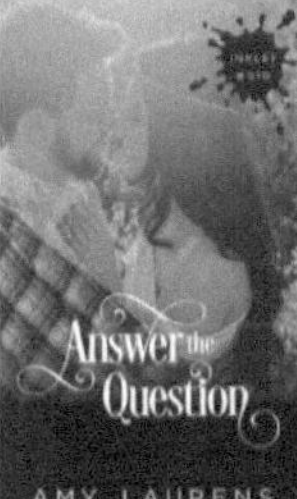

Answer the
Question
AMY LAURENS

Happily
Red
AMY LAURENS

the kitten psychologist
tries to be patient
through email
THEA VAN DIEPEN

DRAGON
Tuesday
AMY LAURENS

RED PLANET
REFUGEES
LIANA BROOKS

the kitten psychologist &
What The Kitten Did
THEA VAN DIEPEN

INKLET #016
Cherry Blossom
AMY LAURENS

INKLET #018
Alone
AMY LAURENS

INKLET #019
the kitten psychologist
& The Kitten
Come To A Conclusion
THEA VAN DIEPEN

INKLET #010
LEVEL NINE
LIANA BROOKS

INKLET #020
To Dust
AMY LAURENS

INKLET #021
Interchange
AMY LAURENS

INKLET #022
Emalia's Lanterns
LIANA BROOKS

INKLET #023
Dear Santa
AMY LAURENS

INKLET #024
The Quilt-Maker's Scrap
AMY L. LAURENS

www.ingramcontent.com/pod-product-compliance
Lightning Source LLC
Chambersburg PA
CBHW051304190726
48286CB00004B/1251